# Happy!

Nancy Carlson

Carolrhoda Books  Minneapolis · New York

To my friend Elaine W.,
who makes friends wherever she goes
(although don't ask her to hold your canoe!)

Feeling sad? Cheer up! Life is a lot more
fun when you **think happy!**

So make yourself happy by looking in the mirror and shouting, "I AM COOL!"

Wear those flashy socks and be
the first kid in school to

**play the
bagpipes.**

# Make Yourself

# Happy

## by speaking up for yourself!

When you can't figure something out,

ask for help.

If a **bully** is bothering you,

remember there is **always**
someone to help you.

# Make Yourself
# Happy
## by having fun!

Play outside
until **dark.**

Throw a **party** or

put on a
**show.**

# Make Yourself Happy

by taking care of your body!

Go for a **bike ride.**

Get a **good night's** sleep.

Drink lots of water because
your body **LOVES** it!

# Make Yourself Happy
## by being friendly!

Wave at your neighbors and guess what?

They'll wave back!

Accept hugs from people who care about you.

And hug them back, because

HUGS JUST FEEL GOOD!

Be the first to say hi to the new kid and . . .

. . . you might find a **new friend**.

# Listen to old folks because they have
## great stories to tell!

# Make Yourself Happy

by staying calm.

Have **faith** and you'll always have
someone to talk to.

**Think happy thoughts when things are tough.**

**When you don't feel lovable,**

When you make yourself happy, something
**really amazing** will happen—

you'll make everyone around you
**happy too!**

Carolrhoda Books
A division of Lerner Publishing Group, Inc.
241 First Avenue North
Minneapolis MN 55401 U.S.A.

Website address: www.lernerbooks.com

Library of Congress Cataloging-in-Publication Data

Carlson, Nancy L.
    Think happy! / by Nancy Carlson.
       p.    cm.
    ISBN 978-0-8225-8940-2 (lib. bdg. : alk. paper)
    1. Happiness—Juvenile literature.  2. Conduct of life—
Juvenile literature.  I. Title.
    BF575.H27C373  2009
    646.7083—dc22                        2008021180

Manufactured in the United States of America
1 2 3 4 5 6 – PA – 14 13 12 11 10 09

EC
6/09